"I have found a kernel of wheat," said the Little Red Hen. **"Now who will help me plant this wheat? Where is that lazy dog? Where is that lazy cat? Where is that lazy mouse?"**

"Wait a minute. Hold everything. You can't tell your story right here. This is the endpaper. The book hasn't even started yet."

"Who are you? Will you help me plant the wheat?"

"I'm Jack. I'm the narrator. And no, I can't help you plant the wheat. I'm a very busy guy trying to put a book together. Now why don't you just disappear for a few pages. I'll call when I need you."

"But who will help me tell my story? Who will help me draw a picture of the wheat? Who will help me spell 'the wheat'?"

"Listen Hen— forget the wheat. Here comes the Title Page!"

Title Page.

(for The Stinky Cheese Man & Other Fairly Stupid Tales)

PUFFIN BOOKS

This book is
dedicated to our
close, personal
special friend:

(your name here)

—J.S. & L.S.

I know. I know.
The page is upside down.
I meant to do that.
Who ever looks at that
dedication stuff anyhow?
If you really want to read
it—you can always stand
on your head.

A long time ago, people used to tell magical stories of wonder and enchantment. Those stories were called Fairy Tales.

Those stories are not in this book. The stories in this book are almost Fairy Tales. But not quite.

The stories in this book are Fairly Stupid Tales.

I mean, what else would you call a story like "Goldilocks and the Three Elephants"? This girl walking through the woods smells Peanut Porridge cooking. She decides to break into the Elephants' house, eat the porridge, sit in the chairs, and sleep in the beds. But when she gets in the house she can't climb up on Baby Elephant's chair because it's too big. She can't climb up on Mama Elephant's chair because it's much too big. And she can't climb up on Papa Elephant's chair because it's much much too big. So she goes home. The End.

And if you don't think that's fairly stupid, you should read "Little Red Running Shorts" or maybe "The Stinky Cheese Man."

In fact, you should definitely go read the stories now, because the rest of this introduction just kind of goes on and on and doesn't really say anything. I stuck it on to the end here so it would fill up the page and make it look like I really knew what I was talking about. So stop now. I mean it. Quit reading. Turn the page. If you read this last sentence, it won't tell you anything.

JACK

Up the Hill
Fairy Tale Forest
1992

SURGEON GENERAL'S WARNING: It has been determined that these tales are fairly stupid and probably dangerous to your health.

Once upon a time Chicken Licken was standing around when a piece of something fell on her head. She wasn't the brightest thing on two legs, so she started running around in circles clucking,
"The sky is falling! The sky is falling!
We must tell the President!"
Chicken Licken ran to her friend Ducky Lucky and clucked, "Ducky Lucky! Ducky Lucky! The sky is falling! The sky is falling! We must tell the President!"
"Let's go," quacked Ducky Lucky.
Chicken Licken and Ducky Lucky ran to their friend Goosey Loosey and yelled, "Goosey Loosey! Goosey Loosey! The sky is falling! The sky is falling!
We must tell the President!"
"Let's go," honked Goosey Loosey.
Chicken Licken, Ducky Lucky, and Goosey Loosey ran to their friend Cocky Locky and yelled, "Cocky Locky! Cocky Locky! The sky is falling!
The sky is falling! We must tell the President!"
"Let's go," crowed Cocky Locky.

"Wait a minute! Wait a minute!" cried Jack the Narrator. "I forgot the Table of Contents! I forgot the Table of Contents!"

"Hey, you're not in this story," said Chicken Licken.

"I know," said Jack the Narrator. "But I came to warn you. The Table of Contents is—"

"The sky is falling! The sky is falling!" clucked Chicken Licken. "We must tell the President!"

So Chicken Licken, Ducky Lucky, Goosey Loosey, and Cocky Locky ignored Jack the Narrator and ran off to catch a plane to Washington.

Just outside the airport they met Foxy Loxy.

"Foxy Loxy! Foxy Loxy! The sky is falling! The sky is falling! We must tell the President!" yelled Chicken Licken, Ducky Lucky, Goosey Loosey, and Cocky Locky.

"Well, come with me," said Foxy Loxy. "I know a shortcut to the airport."

Foxy Loxy led Chicken Licken, Ducky Lucky, Goosey Loosey, and Cocky Locky to his cave. He didn't get to eat them though, because Chicken Licken was almost right. The sky wasn't falling.

The Table of
Contents was.
It fell and
squashed
everybody.
The End.

TABLE OF CONTENTS

Chicken Licken

4

The Princess and the Bowling Ball   10

The Really Ugly Duckling

The Other Frog Prince

16

Little Red Running Shorts

Jack's Bean Problem   18

Cinderumpelstiltskin   22

The Tortoise and the Hair

The Stinky   28

Cheese Man   30

48

 The Boy Who Cried "Cow Patty"   52

Once upon a time there was a Prince. And this Prince's dad and mom (the King and Queen) somehow got it into their royal heads that no Princess would be good enough for their boy unless she could feel a pea through one hundred mattresses.

So it should come as no surprise that the Prince had a very hard time finding a Princess. Every time he met a nice girl, his mom and dad would pile one hundred mattresses on top of a pea and then invite her to sleep over.

When the Princess came down for breakfast, the Queen would ask, "How did you sleep, dear?"

The Princess would politely say, "Fine, thank you."

And the King would show her the door.

Now this went on for three years. And of course nobody ever felt the pea under one hundred mattresses. Then one day the Prince met the girl of his dreams. He decided he better do something about it. That night, before the Princess went to bed, the Prince slipped his bowling ball under the one hundred mattresses.

When the Princess came down for breakfast the next morning, the Queen asked, "How did you sleep, dear?"

"This might sound odd," said the Princess. "But I think you need another mattress. I felt like I was sleeping on a lump as big as a bowling ball."

The King and Queen were satisfied.

The Prince and Princess were married.

And everyone lived happily, though maybe not completely honestly, ever after. The End.

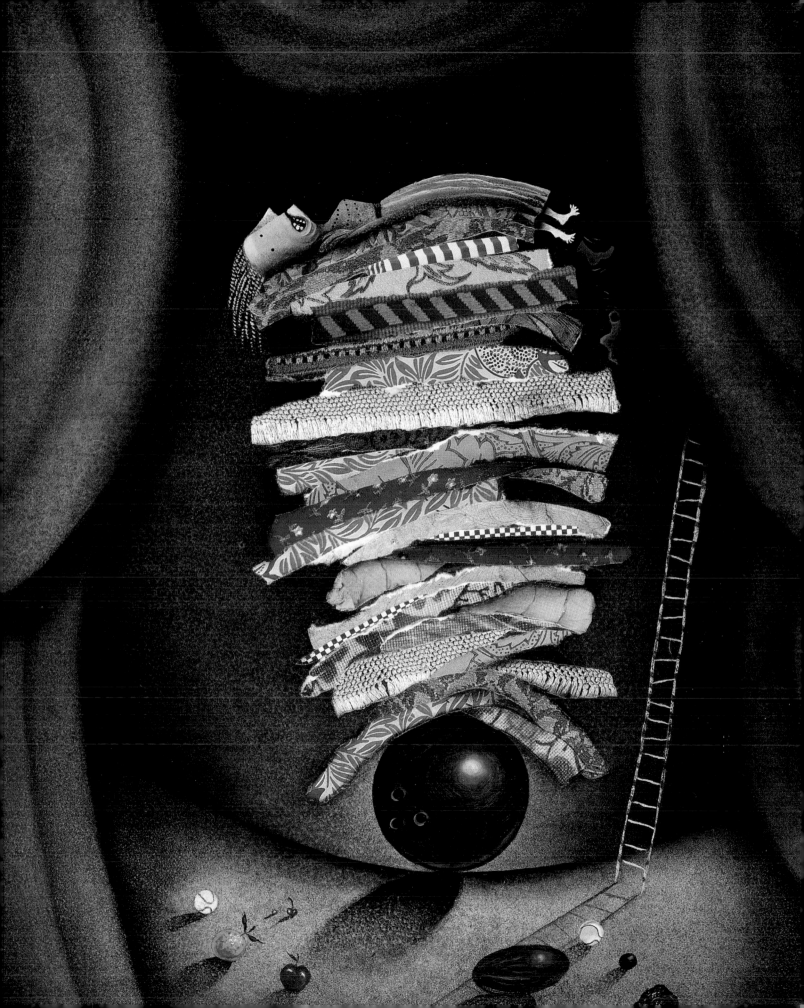

Once upon a time there was a mother duck and a father duck who had seven baby ducklings. Six of them were regular-looking ducklings. The seventh was a really ugly duckling. Everyone used to say, "What a nice-looking bunch of ducklings—all except that one. Boy, he's really ugly." The really ugly duckling heard these people, but he didn't care. He knew that one day he would probably grow up to be a swan and be bigger and look better than anything in the pond.

Well, as it turned out, he was just a really ugly duckling. And he grew up to be just a really ugly duck. The End.

Once upon a time there was a frog.

One day when he was sitting on his lily pad, he saw a beautiful princess sitting by the pond. He hopped in the water, swam over to her, and poked his head out of the weeds.

"Pardon me, O beautiful princess," he said in his most sad and pathetic voice. "I wonder if you could help me."

The princess was about to jump up and run, but she felt sorry for the frog with the sad and pathetic voice.

Rhyssa persuasoria

stellifera

fly

So she asked, "What can I do to help you, little frog?"
"Well," said the frog. "I'm not really a frog, but a handsome prince
who was turned into a frog by a wicked witch's spell. And the spell
can only be broken by the kiss of a beautiful princess."
The princess thought about this for a second, then lifted the frog from
the pond and kissed him.
"I was just kidding," said the frog. He jumped back into the pond and
the princess wiped the frog slime off her lips. The End.

"Okay, I've got things running smoothly now," said Jack the Narrator. "And this next story is even better than the last three. See, it's about this girl who runs very fast and always wears red running shorts. That's where her name comes from, get it? So anyway, this girl is running to her granny's house when she meets a wolf. He tricks her into taking the long way while he takes the shortcut. Now this is the good part because Red runs so fast that she beats the wolf to granny's house. He knocks on the door. Red answers it. And guess what she says? 'My, what slow feet you have.' And that's it. *The End*. Is that great or what? So sit back, relax, and enjoy—'Little Red Running Shorts.'

"And now, like I already said—'Little Red Running Shorts.'"

"You just told the whole story," says Little Red Running Shorts.

"We're not going to tell it again."

"You can't say that," says Jack. "You have to start with 'Once upon a time.'"

"No way," says the wolf. "You blew it."

"But you guys are next. Look at the title at the top of the page—'Little Red Running Shorts.' That's you."

"Let's go, Wolf. We're out of here."

"Wait. You can't do this. Your story is supposed to be three pages long. What do I do when we turn the page?"

"I planted the wheat. I watered the wheat. I harvested the wheat. Now do I get to tell my story?" said the Little Red Hen. "Say, what's going on here? Why is that page blank? Is that my page? Where is that lazy dog? Where is that lazy cat? Where is that lazy mouse? How do they expect me to tell the whole story by myself? Where is that lazy narrator? Where is that lazy illustrator? Where is that lazy author?"

"Forget that **Hen.**
Now it's time for the best
story in the whole book——my
story. Because Once Upon a
Time I traded our last cow
for three magic beans and…
hey, Giant. What are you
doing down here? You're
wrecking my whole story."
"I DON'T LIKE THAT
STORY," said the Giant.
"YOU ALWAYS
TRICK ME."
"That's the best part,"
said Jack.
"FEE FI FUM FORY.
I HAVE MADE MY
OWN STORY."
      "Great rhyme, Giant. And
I'm sure your story is just as
good. But there's no room for
it. So why don't you climb
back up the beanstalk. I'll
be up in a few minutes to
        steal your gold and your
            singing harp."

"I'LL GRIND YOUR BONES TO MAKE MY BREAD."

"I knew you'd understand. And there's another little thing that's been bugging me. Could you please stop talking in uppercase letters? It really messes up the page."

"I WILL READ MY STORY NOW,"

said the Giant. And he did.

THE END

of the evil Stepmother

said "I'll HUFF and SNUFF and

give you three wishes."

The beast changed into

SEVEN DWARVES

HAPPILY EVER AFTER

for a spell had been cast by a Wicked Witch

Once upon a time

"That's your story?" said Jack.
"You've got to be kidding. That's not a
Fairly Stupid Tale. That's an Incredibly Stupid Tale.
That's an Unbelievably Stupid Tale. That is
the Most Stupid Tale I Ever— *awwwk!*"
The Giant grabbed Jack and dragged him to the next page.

Once upon a time there was a Giant. The Giant squeezed Jack and said, "TELL ME A BETTER STORY OR I WILL GRIND YOUR BONES TO MAKE MY BREAD. AND WHEN YOUR STORY IS FINISHED, I WILL GRIND YOUR BONES TO MAKE MY BREAD ANYWAY! HO, HO, HO." The Giant laughed an ugly laugh. Jack thought, "He'll kill me if I do. He'll kill me if I don't. There's only one way to get out of this." Jack cleared his throat, and then began his story.

Once upon a time there was a Giant. The Giant squeezed Jack and said, "TELL ME A BETTER STORY OR I WILL GRIND YOUR BONES TO MAKE MY BREAD. AND WHEN YOUR STORY IS FINISHED, I WILL GRIND YOUR BONES TO MAKE MY BREAD ANYWAY! HO, HO, HO." The Giant laughed an ugly laugh. Jack thought, "He'll kill me if I do. He'll kill me if I don't. There's only one way to get out of this." Jack cleared his throat, and then began his story. Once upon a time there was a Giant. The Giant squeezed Jack and said, "TELL ME A BETTER STORY OR I WILL GRIND YOUR BONES TO MAKE MY BREAD. AND WHEN YOUR STORY IS FINISHED, I WILL GRIND YOUR BONES TO MAKE MY BREAD ANYWAY! HO, HO, HO." The Giant laughed an ugly laugh. Jack thought, "He'll kill me if I do. He'll kill me if I don't. There's only one way to get out of this." Jack cleared his throat, and then began his story. Once upon a time there was a Giant. The Giant squeezed Jack and said, "TELL ME A BETTER STORY OR I WILL GRIND YOUR BONES TO MAKE MY BREAD. AND WHEN YOUR STORY IS FINISHED, I WILL GRIND YOUR BONES TO MAKE MY BREAD ANYWAY! HO, HO, HO." The Giant laughed an ugly laugh. Jack thought, "He'll kill me if I do. He'll kill me if I don't. There's only one way to get out of this." Jack cleared his throat, and then began his story. Once upon a time there was a Giant. The Giant squeezed Jack and said, "TELL ME A BETTER STORY OR I WILL GRIND YOUR BONES TO MAKE MY BREAD. AND WHEN YOUR STORY IS FINISHED, I WILL GRIND YOUR BONES TO MAKE MY BREAD ANYWAY! HO, HO, HO." The Giant laughed an ugly laugh. Jack thought, "He'll kill me if I do. He'll kill me if I don't. There's only one way to get out of this." Jack cleared his throat, and then began his story. Once upon a time there was a Giant. The Giant squeezed Jack and said, "TELL ME A BETTER STORY OR I WILL GRIND YOUR BONES TO MAKE MY BREAD. AND WHEN YOUR STORY IS FINISHED, I WILL GRIND YOUR BONES TO MAKE MY BREAD ANYWAY! HO, HO, HO." The Giant laughed an ugly laugh. Jack thought, "He'll kill me if I do. He'll kill me if I don't. There's only one way to get out of this." Jack cleared his throat, and then began his story. Once upon a time there was a Giant. The Giant squeezed Jack and said, "TELL ME A BETTER STORY OR I WILL GRIND YOUR BONES TO MAKE MY BREAD. AND WHEN YOUR STORY IS FINISHED, I WILL GRIND YOUR BONES TO MAKE MY BREAD ANYWAY! HO, HO, HO." The Giant laughed an ugly laugh. Jack thought, "He'll kill me if I do. He'll kill me if I don't. There's only one way to get out of this." Jack cleared his throat, and then began his story. Once upon a time there was a Giant. The Giant squeezed Jack and said, "TELL ME A BETTER STORY OR I WILL GRIND YOUR BONES TO MAKE MY BREAD. AND WHEN YOUR STORY IS FINISHED, I WILL GRIND YOUR BONES TO MAKE MY BREAD ANYWAY! HO, HO, HO." The Giant laughed an ugly laugh. Jack thought, "He'll kill me if I do. He'll kill me if I don't. There's only one way to

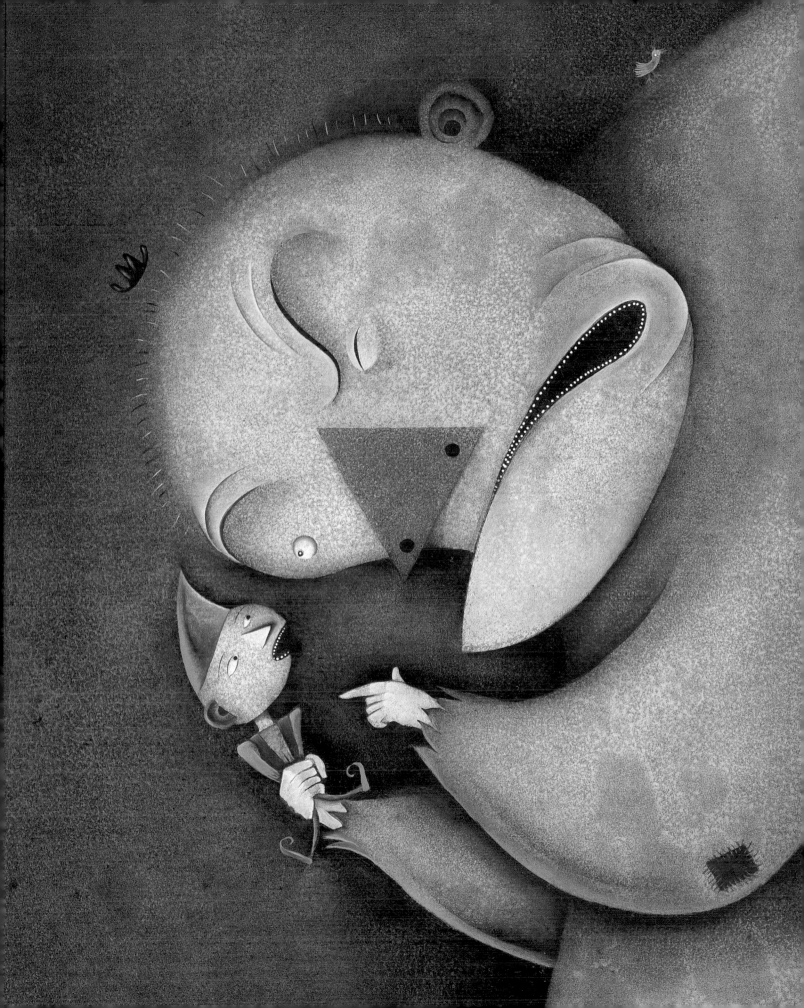

Once upon a time there was a beautiful girl named Cinderella who lived with her wicked stepmother and two ugly stepsisters. These steprelatives were not only wicked and ugly—they also made Cinderella clean the house every day.

One day the local prince announced that he was holding a fabulous ball at his castle. Everyone was invited.

The stepmother and stepsisters got all dressed up to go. But, as usual, they made Cinderella clean the house, so she didn't have time to get ready. After the stepmother and stepsisters left for the ball, Cinderella sat down and began to cry.

Just then a little man appeared.

"Please don't cry," he said. "I can help you spin straw into gold."

"I don't think that will do me much good," said Cinderella. "I need a fancy dress, glass slippers, and a coach."

"Would you like to try to guess my name?" said the clever little man.

Cinderella looked at him. "No. Not really."

"Come on. Do you think it's 'Chester'?"

"If you don't have a dress, it doesn't really matter."

"Oh, just guess a name, any name."

"I'm not supposed to talk to strangers," said Cinderella. Then she closed the door and left the little man standing outside screaming, "RUMPELSTILTSKIN! RUMPELSTILTSKIN! RUMPELSTILTSKIN!"

When the stepmother and stepsisters got home from the ball, Cinderella told them about the strange little man. They still made her clean the house. And meaner still, they changed her name to Cinderumpelstiltskin. The End.

Once upon a time there was a Tortoise
who was very slow but very dependable.
He would always get where he set out to go.
It just took him longer than most people.
One day Rabbit saw Tortoise walking
slowly but surely down the road and said,
"Tortoise, you are so slow. I could
probably grow hair faster than you run."
"Oh yeah?" said Tortoise slowly.
"Yeah," said Rabbit.
So they decided to race.
On the day of the big race Tortoise and
Rabbit lined up at the starting line.
Owl said, "On your mark. Get set. Grow!"
Tortoise started to run.
Rabbit started to grow his hair.

Tortoise ran. Rabbit grew his hair. Tortoise ran. Rabbit grew his hair. Tortoise ran. Rabbit grew his hair. Tortoise ran. Rabbit grew his hair. Tortoise ran. Rabbit grew his hair. Tortoise ran. Rabbit grew his hair. Tortoise is still running. Rabbit is still growing his hair. *Not* The End.

Once upon a time there was a little old woman and a little old man who lived together in a little old house.

They were lonely. So the little old lady decided to make a man out of stinky cheese.

She gave him a piece of bacon for a mouth and two olives for eyes and put him in the oven to cook.

When she opened the oven to see if he was done, the smell knocked her back. "Phew! What is that terrible smell?" she cried. The Stinky Cheese Man hopped out of the oven and ran out the door calling, "Run run run as fast as you can. You can't catch me. I'm the Stinky Cheese Man!"

The little old lady and the little old man sniffed the air. "I'm not really very hungry," said the little old man. "I'm not really all that lonely," said the little old lady. So they didn't chase the Stinky Cheese Man. The Stinky Cheese Man ran and ran until he met a cow eating grass in a field. "Wow! What's that awful smell?" said the cow.

The Stinky Cheese Man said,
"I've run away from a little old lady
and a little old man and I can run
away from you too I can. Run run run
as fast as you can. You can't catch me.
I'm the Stinky Cheese Man!"
The cow gave another sniff and said,
"I'll bet you could give someone
two or three stomachaches.
I think I'll just eat weeds."
So the cow didn't chase
the Stinky Cheese Man either.
The Stinky Cheese Man ran and ran
until he met some kids playing
outside school.
"Gross," said a little girl.
"What's that nasty smell?"
"I've run away from a little old lady,
and a little old man, and a cow, and
I can run away from you too I can.
Run run run as fast as you can.
You can't catch me.
I'm the Stinky Cheese Man!"
A little boy looked up, sniffed the
air and said, "If we catch him, our
teacher will probably make us eat
him. Let's get out of here."
So the kids didn't chase
the Stinky Cheese Man either.

By and by the Stinky Cheese Man
came to a river with no bridge.
"How will I ever cross this river?
It's too big to jump, and if I try to swim
across I'll probably fall apart,"
said You-Know-Who.
Just then the sly fox (who shows up in
a lot of stories like these) poked his head
out of the bushes.
"Why, just hop on my back and I'll
carry you across, Stinky Cheese Man."
"How do I know you won't eat me?"
"Trust me," said the fox.
So the Stinky Cheese Man hopped on
the fox's back.
The fox swam to the middle of the
river and said, "Oh man! What is that
funky smell?"

The fox coughed, gagged, and sneezed, and the Stinky Cheese Man flew off his back and into the river

where he fell apart. The End.

"Shhhhh. Be very quiet. I moved the endpaper up here so the Giant would think the book is over. The big lug is finally asleep. Now I can sneak out of here. Just turn the page very quietly and that will be The…

"I found the wheat.
I planted the wheat. I grew
the wheat. I harvested the
wheat. I ground the wheat.
I made the dough. I baked
the bread," said the Little
Red Hen. "And did anyone
help me? Did anyone
save space for my story?
So now," said the Little
Red Hen, "who
thinks they're
going to help
me EAT the
BREAD?"

"BREAD?" said the Giant.
"EAT?" said the Giant.

PUFFIN BOOKS

Published by the Penguin Group
Penguin Books Ltd, 27 Wrights Lane, London W8 5TZ, England
Penguin Books USA Inc., 375 Hudson Street, New York, New York 10014, USA
Penguin Books Australia Ltd, Ringwood, Victoria, Australia
Penguin Books Canada Ltd, 10 Alcorn Avenue, Toronto, Ontario, Canada M4V 3B2
Penguin Books (NZ) Ltd, 182-190 Wairau Road, Auckland 10, New Zealand

Penguin Books Ltd, Registered Offices: Harmondsworth, Middlesex, England

First published in the United States of America by Viking Penguin,
a division of Penguin Books USA Inc. 1992
First published in Great Britain in Picture Puffins 1993
10 9 8 7 6 5

Filmset in Bodoni

Made and printed in Italy by Printers srl – Trento

The illustrations are rendered in oil and vinegar

Design: Molly Leach, New York, New York